This book belongs to the
❀ Webbers

THAT'S NOT FAIR

BY GINA AND MERCER MAYER

A GOLDEN BOOK • NEW YORK

Western Publishing Company, Inc., Racine, Wisconsin 53404

Sometimes things just aren't fair.

I had to make my bed. That wasn't fair. It was just going to get messed up again.

I wanted to give my sister a haircut,
but Mom said, "No, you can't."
That wasn't fair.

So I gave my sister's doll
a haircut instead.

I wanted to eat watermelon in the
living room, but Mom made me go
back in the kitchen. That wasn't fair.

We went to the mall to get me some new clothes. I didn't want new clothes.

I wanted to go to the toy store,
but Mom said, "Not now."

I had to try on a pair of pants
and a sweater.

I wanted to get an ice cream cone, but Mom said, "We don't have time."

1000 FLAVORS

So I asked to go to the candy store instead. We couldn't do that either.

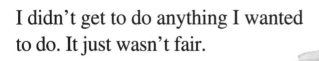

I didn't get to do anything I wanted to do. It just wasn't fair.

On the way home, I turned on my
ray gun. Dad made me stop because
the baby was sleeping.
I said, "That's not fair."
Dad said, "Things aren't always fair."

Later, when I made a tent out of Mom's bedspread, Mom said, "You have a tent outside."

I said, "I don't want to play outside."
I had to go out anyway. Was that fair?

I found a skunk in the garden. I wanted to
bring him in the house to feed him,
but Mom and Dad screamed, "No!"
That wasn't fair. The skunk was
really hungry.

I wanted to take my brother for
a bike ride, but Mom said he
was too little.
He wanted to go. It wasn't fair.

Later Dad made me give the dog
a bath. That wasn't fair. My dog
likes to be dirty.

At dinner I ate all my carrots, but
I had to take out the trash anyway.
I knew that wasn't fair.

Then *I* had to take a bath. That
wasn't fair. I like to be dirty, too.

When I wanted to finger-paint, Dad
said, "Not now—you've just had a bath."
I got mad. I yelled, "That's not fair!"
Dad made me go to my room
until I said I was sorry.

I said I was sorry even though
it wasn't fair. I just wanted to
watch TV.

Mom and Dad say that sometimes things just aren't fair. But there is one thing that I know *is* fair . . .

I get to stay up later than my sister
and brother every single night.